Praise for ♥ One Love

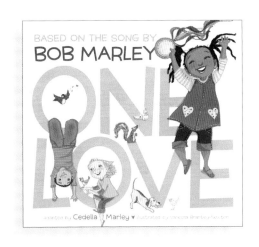

'A heart-warming book to read or sing as you share it together.'
– *Junior Magazine*

'A feel-good story of a community coming together.'
– *Publishers Weekly*

'Deceptively simple and brilliantly executed.'
– *School Library Journal*

Praise for Every Little Thing

'Will strike a chord with worrywarts and loving children everywhere.'
– *School Library Journal*

Praise for Get Up, Stand Up

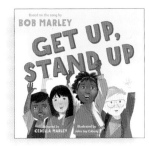

'A message of empowerment and unity . . . Joyous.'
– *Kirkus Reviews*

'Carrying on her father's legacy of banding people together in solidarity, Cedella Marley adds to her collection of picture book adaptations of the singer-songwriter's beloved work with this new installment. An energetic read-aloud that promises to pump up young dissenters and peacemakers.'
– *Publishers Weekly*

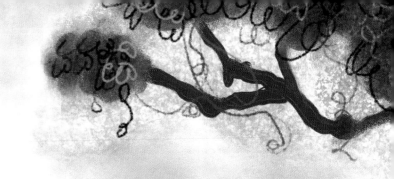

• • • TO
MY THREE SONS;
SOUL REBEL, SKIP AND
SAIYAN, YOU ARE MY EVERY-
THING EVERY DAY. AND FOR BOBBY,
OUR VERY SPECIAL CHOCOLATE LAB
WHO BROUGHT US SO MUCH LOVE.
– C. M.

• • • TO
HASHEM AND FOR
MY COMMUNITY WITH
WHOM I SHARE ONE LOVE:
RAY, COY, LORI, ERIC, LORDEAN,
ILENE AND YVONNE. THANKS FOR
THE LOVE AND PRAYERS, NESTER.
– V. N.

• • •

First paperback edition published in 2021
by Chronicle Books LLC.
Originally published in hardcover in 2011
by Chronicle Books LLC.

• • •

Text © 2011 by Cedella Marley.
Illustrations © 2011 by Vanessa Brantley-Newton.

• • •

ISBN 978-1-7972-1186-2

• • •

Manufactured in China.

• • •

Original book design by Kristine Brogno.
Paperback design by Sara Gillingham Studio.
Typeset in Family Cat, Family Cat Fat and Gotham.
The illustrations in this book were rendered
in mixed media and digitally.

• • •

10 9 8 7 6 5 4 3 2 1

• • •

Chronicle Books LLC
680 Second Street
San Francisco, California
94107

Chronicle Books – we see things differently.
Become part of our community at
www.chroniclekids.com.

TUFF
GONG

BASED ON THE SONG BY
BOB MARLEY

ONE
LOVE

adapted by **Cedella Marley** ♥ illustrated by Vanessa Brantley-Newton

chronicle books · san francisco

One love,
one heart,
let's get together
and feel all right!

One love,
what my family
gives to me.

One love,

what the flower
gives the bee.

One love,

what Mother Earth
gives the tree.

One love,
one heart,

let's get together and feel all right!

One heart,
    like the birds,
I long to be free.

One love,
 like the river
  runs to the sea.

One heart,

like the music,
    just feel the beat.

Let's get together and feel all right!

One love,
         when your hand
reaches out for me.

One heart, when we touch,

a new world we'll see.

One love, one heart,

One
Love
Park

let's get together and feel all right!

'One love, one heart, let's get together and feel all right.'

Simple and true – but it seems to be the hardest thing to do. From my parents' humble beginnings in Jamaica's Trench Town, the one thing they always instilled in us was, and still is, love.

My father once said, 'Children is wonderful, a part of my richness.' The richness was not monetary but rather the joy he felt in his heart when he looked upon his children. I feel the same thing every time I look at my three boys. So when I started to adapt his song 'One Love' as the basis for this picture book, I knew, at once, it would be a heartfelt project.

I think everybody has a 'happy song' and 'One Love' is mine. Yet, in many ways, it's everybody's happy song. It's also a healing song, and I played it for my boys when they weren't feeling well. 'One Love' is also a great 'sleepy-time song'. I remember humming it softly as I cuddled with my boys on those nights when nothing else worked for them . . . or me.

When my father sang 'One Love', he felt it all the way – heart and soul, mind and body. He thought a world united by love was possible, and it is. All we've got to do, he said, is 'Give a little, take a little.' My father wanted people to embrace one another and take care of one another. That was and is the message of 'One Love', And I have tried to pass that message of love and community to all of the readers of this book.

I hope 'One Love' will be your 'happy-healing-sleepy' song because I know it can do for you what it has always done for me and my kids.

One love to everyone!

Cedella Marley

Bob Marley (1945–1981)

was a Jamaican singer-songwriter and musician. He remains the most widely known performer of reggae music. In 1994 Marley was inducted into the Rock and Roll Hall of Fame; in 1999 *Time* magazine chose Bob Marley & The Wailers' *Exodus* as the greatest album of the twentieth century ('One Love' is on that album); and in 2001 Bob Marley was posthumously awarded the Grammy Lifetime Achievement Award. In 1999 'One Love' was named song of the millennium by the BBC.

Cedella Marley's

life has always been rooted in music and culture. As the oldest child of Bob Marley, she has dedicated herself to keeping her father's message and memory alive. She is a musician as well, performing internationally with the three-time Grammy Award-winning Melody Makers, which consists of her brothers Ziggy and Steve and her sister Sharon. Cedella lives in Florida, with her husband and three sons.

Vanessa Brantley-Newton

is the author and illustrator of *Let Freedom Sing* and *Don't Let Auntie Mabel Bless the Table*. She loves to craft, cook, collect vintage children's books, tell stories, make dolls and shop. She lives in New Jersey, with her husband, daughter and two crazy cats, Kirby and Stripes.